CB137302

JANE AUSTEN

Children's Stories

Dados Internacionais de Catalogação na Publicação (CIP) de acordo com ISBD

A933p Austen, Jane
Pride and prejudice / Jane Austen. – Jandira : W. Books, 2025.
96 p. ; 12,8cm x 19,8cm. – (Jane Austen Children's Stories)

ISBN: 978-65-5294-184-8

1. Literatura infantojuvenil. 2. Romance. 3. Literatura estrangeira. 4. Literatura inglesa. 5. Amor. 6. Preconceito. 7. Inglaterra. I. Título. II. Série.

2025-592 CDD 028.5
CDU 82-93

Elaborado por Vagner Rodolfo da Silva - CRB-8/9410
Índice para catálogo sistemático:
1. Literatura infantojuvenil 028.5
2. Literatura infantojuvenil 82-93

Jane Austen Children's Stories (Easy Classics)
Text © Sweet Cherry Publishing Limited, 2020
Inside illustrations © Sweet Cherry Publishing Limited, 2020
Cover illustrations © Sweet Cherry Publishing Limited, 2020

The right of Gemma Barder to be identified as the author of this work has been asserted by her in accordance with the Copyright, Design and Patents Act 1988.

© 2025 edition:
Ciranda Cultural Editora e Distribuidora Ltda.

1st edition in 2025
www.cirandacultural.com.br
No part of this publication may be reproduced, stored in a retrieval system, or transmitted in any form or by any means, electronic, mechanical, photocopying, recording, or otherwise, without written permission of the publisher.
This book is a work of fiction. Names, characters, places, and incidents are either the product of the author's imagination or are used fictitiously, and any resemblance to actual persons, living or dead, business establishments, events, or locales is entirely coincidental.

JANE AUSTEN

Pride and Prejudice

W. Books

Chapter 1

Mrs Bennet was in a very good mood. She had just discovered that a rich man called Mr Bingley had rented the largest house in her neighbourhood.

'Why should that be such good news for us?' asked Mr Bennet. He

was trying to read his newspaper and growing tired of his wife's excitement.

'Oh, Mr Bennet!' cried Mrs Bennet. 'Because a single man of good fortune must want a wife! And we have *five* daughters!'

Mr Bennet cleared his throat. 'I see,' he said, smiling at his second eldest daughter, Lizzy.

The Bennets lived in a house called Longbourn. It was not the largest, nor the smallest house in the village. Mr Bennet was calm and well respected. Mrs Bennet was lively and had one goal in life: to see her daughters married.

Jane

Jane was the eldest and prettiest daughter. She was also sweet and kind-hearted. Jane always saw the best in people.

Elizabeth

Lizzy was her father's favourite for her cleverness and quick humour. Lizzy loved to go for walks and spend time with Jane.

Mary

Bookish and serious, Mary spent most of her time practising the piano and reading.

Catherine

Kitty was happy and friendly. She loved nothing more than gossiping with Lydia – although they occasionally argued too.

Lydia

Lydia was the youngest daughter and Mrs Bennet's favourite. Mrs Bennet forgave Lydia's silliness, perhaps because Lydia reminded her so much of herself.

The Bennet family did not have to wait long to meet Mr Bingley. They were at a dance in Meryton when the man himself arrived. He brought with him another gentleman and a lady.

'The famous Mr Bingley!' said Lizzy to her best friend, Charlotte Lucas. 'Who are the people with him?'

Charlotte, who lived near Lizzy with

her father Sir William, replied: 'The lady is Mr Bingley's sister. The gentleman is Mr Darcy. He is Bingley's best friend and owns a lot of land in Derbyshire.'

Lizzy stared at Mr Darcy. He looked displeased with everyone and everything in the room. Mr Bingley, on the other hand, could not have looked happier. He walked over to them.

'May I introduce Mr Bingley,' said Sir William. 'This is Miss Jane Bennet and Miss Elizabeth Bennet.'

'It is so nice to meet you,' replied Mr Bingley with a large smile on his face. 'Miss Bennet, would you care to dance with me?'

Jane blushed and accepted.

Chapter 2

Jane danced two dances with Mr Bingley. Lizzy watched her happily. Her eyes sometimes drifted to Mr Bingley's friend. Mr Darcy was handsome, but his expression was miserable. He had not danced once.

'Come now, Darcy!' said Mr Bingley, when his dance with Jane had come to an end. 'Why won't you dance?'

Lizzy could not help listening in, curious what Mr Darcy would say.

'*You* have been dancing with the only acceptable partner in the room,' he replied.

Mr Bingley grinned. 'Darcy, she is the most beautiful creature I ever beheld!'

Lizzy smiled to herself.

'Look,' continued Mr Bingley. 'There's her sister, Elizabeth. She's very pretty too.'

Lizzy froze and stared straight ahead. She did not want to give away that she had been listening.

'She is tolerable, I suppose,' Darcy said. 'But not pretty enough to tempt me.'

Mr Bingley sighed and walked back to Jane.

Mr Darcy's words hurt. Being called "tolerable" was not a compliment.

However, Lizzy wasn't the sort of person to be down for long. She soon stood up and walked past Mr Darcy, smiling at him as she went. She found Charlotte and retold the story to her, complete with an excellent impression of Mr Darcy's proud voice.

Chapter 3

The dance at Meryton confirmed three things to the Bennets:

1. Mr Bingley was wonderful and had excellent taste. He danced four dances with Jane, after all.

2. Mr Darcy may be even richer than his friend, but he had none of his friendliness and charm.

3. Mr Bingley's sister was far more pleased with herself than anything or anyone in Meryton.

The following night, Sir William Lucas invited Mr Bingley and his friends to dinner and dancing at Lucas Lodge. The Bennets were also invited. Lizzy and Charlotte watched as Mr Bingley and Jane danced together again.

'I am so happy for her,' said Lizzy. 'Although it's a shame Mr Bingley's sister and his friend aren't more likeable.'

At that moment, Mr Darcy and Sir William approached and Lizzy fell silent.

'Miss Elizabeth,' Sir William said. 'Why are you not dancing? Come, Mr Darcy, I am sure you would make an excellent partner for Miss Bennet!'

Lizzy blushed. She could not bear to be refused by Mr Darcy again. 'I thank you, sir,' she said quickly. 'But there is no need.'

'I would be glad to dance with you, Miss Bennet,' said Mr Darcy.

Lizzy blinked. She could not be sure if Mr Darcy was being polite or if he actually wanted to dance with her this time. She decided he was being polite because of Sir William.

‘Thank you,’ she said. ‘But I find it perfectly *tolerable* just to watch.’

There was no doubt that Mr Darcy understood her meaning. He walked away to Miss Bingley. She passed him a glass of punch.

‘You look very thoughtful,’ Miss Bingley said. ‘Are you thinking how awful it would be to spend many evenings in such company?’

‘Not at all,’ said Mr Darcy. ‘I was thinking about a pair of fine eyes in the face of a pretty woman.’

Miss Bingley’s face lit up expectantly. She had often hoped that Mr Darcy might speak of her in such a way.

'Dare I ask whose eyes?' she said.

'Miss Elizabeth Bennet's,' he replied.

The following morning, Jane received a note from Netherfield. It was from Mr Bingley's sister, inviting her to spend the day with them.

'May I use the carriage?' Jane asked, excitedly.

'No, no!' replied Mrs Bennet. 'Go on horseback. Then if it rains, you will have to stay!'

As Mrs Bennet had hoped, it rained. It rained so much that by the time Jane arrived at Netherfield she was soaked. She had not made it halfway through her lunch when she began to feel unwell. By teatime she was lying in a guest room with a fever.

Chapter 4

Jane had been at Netherfield for two days. Elizabeth was beginning to worry.

'I must go and see her,' said Elizabeth.

'She is fine!' insisted Mrs Bennet. She was delighted that Jane was too ill to leave Mr Bingley's house. With any luck she would be there until they were engaged. 'Besides, we are going to have lunch at Lucas Lodge with the officers based here for the winter.'

Elizabeth did not care about flirting with officers. She told her mother that she would walk to Netherfield since they were using the carriage. Her mother, as always, could do little to change her mind.

When Lizzy arrived at Netherfield, her boots and the bottom of her dress were muddy. She was shown into the drawing room where Mr Bingley, Mr Darcy and Miss Bingley were taking tea.

Elizabeth did not care how she looked. She was there to see her sister. However, she could not help but notice the shock on Miss Bingley's face when she saw Elizabeth's dress.

'Goodness, did you walk here?' Miss Bingley asked.

'I did,' replied Elizabeth. 'It is only four miles from Longbourn.' For a moment, no one spoke. 'May I see my sister, please?'

After Elizabeth had seen how unwell Jane was for herself, Mr Bingley insisted that she should stay at Netherfield too. Miss Bingley scolded him later.

'Dear brother, are we to be invaded by all the Bennets in the country?' she

cried. 'Did you see the state of her dress this morning? Mr Darcy, what did you think? I cannot believe you would want *your* sister to behave in such a manner.'

'Certainly not,' said Mr Darcy.

'I imagine her "fine eyes" looked quite tired from the journey,' Miss Bingley said with a smirk.

'Not at all,' he replied. 'They were brightened by the exercise.'

After nearly a week at Netherfield, Jane's fever lifted and she was well enough to go home. Lizzy breathed a sigh of relief as she climbed into the carriage. She longed to spend an evening free of Miss Bingley's attempts to impress Mr Darcy. Jane was less happy to be parted from Netherfield and Lizzy could see that it was hard for Mr Bingley too. There had been talk of a ball being held at Netherfield and Lizzy was sure that it would not be long before it was. If only so that Mr Bingley could dance with her sister again.

Chapter 5

'I hope you have arranged a good dinner for today, my dear,' said Mr Bennet one morning. 'There will be a guest at our table.'

'Who?' asked Mrs Bennet, excited at the idea. 'Is it Mr Bingley?'

'No, it is a person I have never met before,' said Mr Bennet. 'My cousin, Mr Collins.'

Mrs Bennet began to wail. Mr Collins was a distant relative of the Bennet family and the only living male heir to Longbourn. When Mr Bennet died, Longbourn would belong to Mr Collins.

Mr Collins arrived and bowed theatrically to his relations. He had not been at Longbourn for ten minutes before he mentioned that his parsonage was in the grounds of Lady Catherine de Bourgh's estate.

‘My humble home is separated only by a lane from Rosings Park,’ he said. It was clear that Mr Collins was very proud of his connection with the great lady. He talked of little else.

The following morning, Mr Collins asked Mrs Bennet for a private talk. ‘It is my greatest wish,’ began Mr Collins, ‘to get married. Lady Catherine herself told me: “a clergyman should have a wife!”’ He laughed.

Mrs Bennet was not sure what to say in reply.

‘As I am to inherit Longbourn,’ Mr Collins continued, ‘it seems only right that I choose a wife from among those living here.'

Mrs Bennet's heart leapt. If one of her girls married Mr Collins, it meant that Longbourn would stay in her family! After warning him that Jane may soon be engaged, Mrs Bennet gave her approval for Mr Collins to choose any of her other daughters. Mr Collins decided on Lizzy.

It was lucky for Mr Collins that Lizzy did not know of his plan. If she had, she would not have been so willing to let him join her and her sisters on a walk to Meryton. As it was, Mr Collins stuck by

her side for the entire journey. He only stopped talking when Kitty and Lydia spotted two officers they knew.

Captain Denny and Captain Carter looked very smart in their bright red officers' uniforms.

'Allow me to introduce George Wickham,' said Captain Denny. 'He will be an officer soon too.' A handsome third gentleman, not yet

in uniform, bowed and smiled at the ladies. He did not have a chance to speak, however, before Mr Bingley and Mr Darcy appeared on horseback.

'What luck!' said Mr Bingley. 'We were just on our way to Longbourn to enquire after Miss Bennet's health.'

Jane's face lit up at the sight of Mr Bingley. Mr Darcy, however, was staring straight at Mr Wickham. Mr Wickham nodded to him. Then without a word or a nod in return, Mr Darcy turned his horse and left.

Chapter 6

Mrs Bennet's sister, Mrs Phillips, had invited the officers for dinner and cards at her home in Meryton. Lizzy was enjoying herself, even though she could not shake Mr Collins. At last, he

was called away to take part in a game and Lizzy had a moment to herself.

'Would you mind if I joined you?' asked Mr Wickham.

'Of course not,' said Lizzy, smiling. 'How are you finding Meryton?'

'Everyone has been very welcoming,' he replied.

Lizzy would not have called Mr Darcy's cold greeting "welcoming". She had been curious about their connection ever since. As if sensing it, Mr Wickham asked, 'Do you know Mr Darcy well?'

Lizzy sighed. 'As well as I wish to. I find him very disagreeable.'

Mr Wickham smiled. 'Mr Darcy and I grew up together.'

Lizzy was surprised. 'But he did not say a word to you when you met!'

'We are not on friendly terms,' replied Mr Wickham. 'My father worked for Mr Darcy's father. When old Mr Darcy died, he left me a job as the clergyman on Mr Darcy's estate at Pemberley.'

'How generous,' said Lizzy. 'He must have cared for you a great deal.'

'He did. It made Mr Darcy jealous. He refused to give me the job and so I have been forced to find other work – as you see.' He waved a hand at his bright new officers' uniform.

Lizzy had known that Mr Darcy was proud and aloof. But she would never have guessed he could be so *cruel.* Fortunately Mr Wickham seemed to take his misfortune well. His warmth was worth more than Mr Darcy's riches, at least in Lizzy's eyes.

The ball at Netherfield was announced. It was the

biggest event the neighbourhood had seen for a long time. Jane could not wait to see Mr Bingley again and Lizzy was pleased that the officers had been invited too. Her eyes searched for Mr Wickham only to find that he was not there.

Lizzy knew it was because of Mr Darcy and she tried to avoid Mr Darcy's gaze when he approached her. 'Miss Bennet, would you join me for the next dance?'

For a moment, Lizzy was too surprised to speak. She had decided his last invitation was made out of politeness. What was the reason now?

‘Thank you,’ she replied at last. ‘Yes.’

Dancing with Mr Darcy was something Lizzy had vowed she would never do. It annoyed her that she hadn’t been able to think of an excuse not to.

‘When we saw you in Meryton,’ she said as they danced, ‘we had just made a new friend.’

Mr Darcy clenched his jaw, knowing exactly who she was referring to. ‘Mr Wickham is good at making friends,’ he replied.

'Whether he can keep them is less certain.'

'He lost your friendship in a way that he will suffer from all his life,' Lizzy replied.

Mr Darcy's steps faltered a little at hearing this. Lizzy said no more and both were glad when the music stopped and they parted ways.

Chapter 7

The morning after the ball was quiet at Longbourn. Lizzy had found a spot in the parlour to sit and reflect on her dance with Mr Darcy. She still could not make sense of what he had said about Mr Wickham. Then her thoughts were interrupted by her mother.

'Mr Collins would like a word with you, Lizzy. *Alone.*' Mrs Bennet ushered Mr Collins into the parlour and closed the door behind him. Lizzy's eyes widened.

'Elizabeth, almost as soon as I arrived, I chose you as my future wife,' Mr Collins began, to Lizzy's horror. 'It is my wish, and the wish of Lady Catherine, that I marry. I wish to marry you.' Lizzy stood up and

took a step away from him. 'When we are married–'

Lizzy finally found her voice.

'Mr Collins, I haven't given you an answer. Let me do so now. I thank you for your offer, but I cannot marry you.'

Mr Collins decided that Lizzy was being shy and complimented her. After repeating herself several times, Lizzy had no choice but to leave the parlour. Mrs Bennet was listening outside the door.

'You cannot refuse him, Lizzy!' Mrs Bennet demanded. Seizing her daughter's hand, she pulled her into her father's study.

'Whatever is the matter?' asked Mr Bennet, looking up from his book.

'Mr Collins has asked Lizzy to marry him and she has refused!' cried Mrs Bennet.

Mr Bennet slowly put down his book. 'And what am I to do about it?'

'You must *make* her marry him!' said Mrs Bennet. 'Or I shall never see her again!'

Mr Bennet nodded. 'I see,' he said, and looked at his daughter. 'Then you have an unhappy choice ahead of you, Lizzy. Your mother will never see you again if you do not marry Mr Collins … and I will never see you again if you do.'

Mrs Bennet wailed and Lizzy's heart jumped. She could not have imagined a worse fate than marrying Mr Collins and her father had just saved her from it.

Chapter 8

It seemed that Charlotte Lucas was not as picky as Lizzy when it came to husbands. Soon after Lizzy refused Mr Collins, he became engaged to Charlotte. Mrs Bennet was upset with Lizzy for weeks after the Collins' wedding. Things were made worse when Mr Bingley left Netherfield suddenly for London without any plans to return. Miss Bingley wrote to Jane

saying that they would be seeing Mr Darcy's younger sister. Having heard much of the rich and talented Miss Darcy, it was clear that both Mr Bingley's sister and his friend hoped that Mr Bingley would marry her.

Jane's heartbreak was deep but quiet, and Lizzy's own heart ached for her. Meanwhile, Mrs Bennet took the blow hard. She had now missed out on not one but *two* married daughters.

When Charlotte invited Lizzy to go and stay with her and

Mr Collins at his home in Hunsford, Lizzy was grateful to get away. By then Jane had also left to visit their Aunt and Uncle Gardiner in London.

Mr Collins had not lied about his connection with Lady Catherine. On Lizzy's second evening in Hunsford, they were all invited to dine with her.

Rosings Park was the grandest house Lizzy had ever seen. Before dinner, the party sat with Lady Catherine in a large room surrounded by huge paintings.

'We have two more guests joining us for dinner,' said Lady Catherine.

'My dear nephews, Colonel Fitzwilliam and Mr Darcy.'

Lizzy tensed. She had not seen Mr Darcy since the ball at Netherfield. She was certain he would be as sorry to see her as she would be to see him. Luckily, Lizzy was seated next to Colonel Fitzwilliam at dinner. The Colonel proved to be much better company than his cousin, whom she noticed looking at her often.

'You know Darcy well, I hear,' said Colonel Fitzwilliam.

'Not at all,' said Lizzy. 'He did not make many friends in Meryton.'

'Is that so?' smiled Colonel Fitzwilliam. 'That is unfortunate. Darcy is a very good friend to have.'

'You surprise me,' said Lizzy. 'How so?'

'Only recently he saved his friend Mr Bingley from a bad marriage,' said Colonel Fitzwilliam.

Lizzy's heart sank. 'How did he do that?' she asked. She was not sure she really wanted to know the answer.

'He pointed out that the lady's family was a bad match for Mr Bingley and persuaded him to go to London for a while,' said Colonel Fitzwilliam. 'You see? He is a better man than you thought!'

Chapter 9

Lizzy was still upset by Colonel Fitzwilliam's news the following morning. She could not go to church and risk seeing Mr Darcy there. What would she say to the man who had ruined her beloved sister's happiness?

In the end Lizzy stayed home with a pretend headache, and chased the same thoughts through her head until it really did hurt. How could Mr Darcy be so unkind to Jane? How could he be so cruel to his own best friend as to separate Mr Bingley from the woman he clearly loved?

Lizzy was interrupted by the front door. Mr Darcy himself had come to see her.

'Forgive the intrusion, I hope you are feeling better,' Mr Darcy began.

'A little,' Lizzy lied.

A silence followed. Mr Darcy seemed uncomfortable and would not settle in one place. Lizzy was about to offer him some tea when he stood up again and paced the room.

'It is no good,' Mr Darcy said at last. 'My feelings cannot be denied.

You must allow me to tell you how deeply I admire and love you.'

Lizzy was astonished. As much as she disliked Mr Darcy, she knew it was a great compliment for a gentleman of his high position to say this to her.

'It goes against my family's wishes and my own better judgement,' Mr Darcy continued. 'The low position of your family makes a marriage between us unfortunate but it cannot be helped. You must ease my pain and agree to be my wife.'

Lizzy swallowed her anger. 'I cannot agree,'

she replied. 'Nor can I thank you for your proposal since you have made it so unwillingly.'

Lizzy hoped Mr Darcy would leave, but he did not. 'Is this all the answer I am to expect?' he asked. Lizzy wondered if it was the first time anyone had said no to him.

'It is,' she replied.

Mr Darcy frowned. 'I would like to know why you are rejecting me with so little effort at politeness.'

'And *I* would like to know why you told me that you loved me while insulting my family!' Lizzy shook her head. 'Yet it does not matter. However you had told me, my answer would have been the same. I could never

marry the man who ruined the hopes of my dearest sister.'

Mr Darcy flushed red but he did not deny it.

'A man,' Lizzy continued, 'who could treat Mr Wickham as badly as you have.'

Mr Darcy's expression changed from confusion and disappointment to anger. 'If this is truly what you think of me, Miss Bennet, I shall leave you.' And he did.

Chapter 10

Lizzy did not expect to hear from Mr Darcy again. However the following morning, she received a letter from him.

Miss Bennet,

Do not worry. This letter does not repeat the offer of marriage which was so disgusting to you yesterday. Instead I wish to tell you the truth about my connection to George Wickham.

When my father died, Mr Wickham was given the job of clergyman at the church on my estate at Pemberley. He turned down the job and was given £1000 instead. I did not hear from him again until last summer when my sister, Georgiana, went missing. Mr Wickham had convinced her that he was in love with her and they had run away to marry. However, when I found them, Wickham admitted that all he wanted was my sister's money.

On the subject of your own sister, Miss Jane Bennet, I admit that I told Mr Bingley she was not in love with him. I had watched her carefully and I could not see any special affection for him. I was worried that she, like your mother, might care more for his money. I acted to protect my friend.

Yours,

Fitzwilliam Darcy

Lizzy was relieved to finally go home to Longbourn. Her mind was still full of Mr Darcy's letter and she longed for her family to distract her.

Lydia was excited because she had been invited to Brighton with one of the officer's wives. Kitty was upset that she hadn't been invited too. Mary could not care less. Jane was quiet.

Life continued this way until the arrival of Mrs Bennet's brother and his wife. Mr and Mrs Gardiner were on their way to Derbyshire for a holiday. Lizzy was excited to be invited along. She had read about Derbyshire and could not wait to explore its sights.

'There is one place I would very much like to see,' said Mrs Gardiner during their trip. 'Pemberley is not far from here.'

'We could not visit without an invitation,' said Lizzy. She blushed at the thought of visiting the house that would have been her own if she had agreed to marry Mr Darcy.

'The family are away at the moment,' said Mr Gardiner. 'The housekeeper is happy to show visitors around.'

Lizzy nodded. She had to admit that she was curious to see Pemberley.

Chapter 11

Pemberley was more beautiful than Lizzy had ever imagined. Inside, the housekeeper showed them a portrait of Mr Darcy and

was excited to hear that Lizzy had met him.

'Isn't he a handsome man?' asked the housekeeper.

Lizzy blushed a little. 'Yes,' she replied. 'Very handsome.'

'He is kind, too,' said the housekeeper. 'Let me show you the piano he bought for his sister …'

Lizzy wondered at this "kind" version of Darcy as she explored the gardens. She was so lost in her thoughts that she almost walked into the man himself.

'Miss Bennet!' said Mr Darcy, shocked to see her.

'Mr Darcy! Forgive me. We thought you were away from home or we would never have come.'

'I returned a day early,' he said. 'Are you staying in Derbyshire?'

'Yes, with my aunt and uncle,' Lizzy said.

'I would like to meet them,' said Darcy.

Mr Darcy seemed friendlier and happier than Lizzy had ever seen him. Perhaps it was because he was in his own home, or perhaps Lizzy just knew him better now.

He invited Lizzy and the Gardiners to dinner the following evening.

'My sister would very much like to meet you,' he said.

'I would like to meet her,' said Lizzy.

Georgiana Darcy was a sweet girl. She was shy but played the piano beautifully when Lizzy encouraged her. Lizzy could easily see how someone like Mr Wickham could have fooled her.

'My brother speaks very highly of you,' said Georgiana as she played.

'I do not know why!' laughed Lizzy.

'You must be a good person. My brother is an excellent judge of character.'

Lizzy looked over to Mr Darcy. He was talking with her aunt and uncle but he looked up just then and smiled at her. Lizzy smiled back.

Chapter 12

Lizzy received two letters from Jane at the hotel where she was staying.

'You stay here and read your letters,' said Mr Gardiner. 'We'll walk to the church and come back for you later.'

Lizzy was eager to hear the news from home and tore into the first letter. It began normally, but halfway through it changed.

Lizzy, since writing the above we have had some shocking news. Lydia has left Brighton for Scotland. She has run away with Mr Wickham! She left a note with her friend to say that they are to be married.

I will write again when I have more news.

Jane

Lizzy's hands were trembling as she opened the second letter.

Dearest Lizzy,
I have more bad news. As foolish as a marriage would have been, we now believe that it has not even happened! Lydia and Mr Wickham are hiding in London now and our father has gone to look for them. Mother begs you to ask Uncle Gardiner to come and help.

Please return home as soon as you get this letter.

Jane

'Oh, Lydia!' cried Lizzy. She did not want Wickham as part of her family, but he *must* marry Lydia now that they had been living together. Their family would be ruined if he did not. However Wickham cared only about marrying someone with money and Lydia had none.

As Lizzy ran towards the door, Mr Darcy entered. He looked at Lizzy's tears with concern.

'Whatever is the matter?' he asked. 'Are you unwell?'

'No, no,' replied Lizzy. 'But I must find my uncle at once!'

Mr Darcy forced Lizzy to sit down. He sent a boy from the hotel to fetch Mr Gardiner and asked Lizzy to explain.

'My sister, Lydia,' Lizzy managed between sobs, 'has run away with Mr Wickham!'

Mr Darcy did not stay for long. Lizzy was sure he wished to escape the embarrassing matter as soon as possible. The Gardiners left for Longbourn. Mr Bennet had not found Lydia and it was left for Mr Gardiner to continue the search.

A week later, Mr Bennet received a letter from London. He showed it to Lizzy.

My dear brother-in-law,
Lydia and Mr Wickham
were married this morning.
Mr Wickham is going to move
to Newcastle and they will visit
Longbourn on the way.
Mr Gardiner

'They are married!' cried Lizzy.

Mr Bennet did not look as relieved as his daughter. 'A man like Wickham would have demanded a lot of money before he agreed to marry Lydia,' he said. 'The question is how much? And how can I ever repay your uncle ...'

Chapter 13

When Lydia returned to Longbourn as Mrs Wickham, she was not at all sorry for what she had done. Mrs Bennet only cared that one of her daughters was married.

'Of course, I wish we had been married here so you could all have been bridesmaids,' Lydia told her sisters. 'In the end, only our aunt and uncle and Mr Darcy were there.'

'Mr Darcy?' Lizzy gasped. 'What on earth was he doing at your wedding?'

'It was Darcy who found us in London,' giggled Lydia.

Lizzy swallowed. If Mr Darcy had found them, then it must be he who had paid Wickham to marry Lydia. Her family had been saved by Mr Darcy.

Lizzy was happy when the Wickhams' visit was over. She felt as though her family had been battered by a storm. What they needed now was calm.

Unfortunately, Mrs Bennet was anything but calm when Mr Bingley returned to Meryton and came to Longbourn with Mr Darcy. As they sat drinking tea, Lizzy longed to thank Mr Darcy for what he had

done for her family. Even if she could have, Mrs Bennet's chatter left no room for anyone, including Mr Bingley, to say anything.

On his second visit, Mr Bingley came alone. He asked to talk to Jane privately.

As everyone had predicted, Mr Bingley was still in love with Jane. He asked her to marry him and Jane was the happiest woman alive – although Mrs Bennet came a close second.

Chapter 14

The very next day, Mrs Bennet was already planning Jane's wedding outfit when a huge carriage arrived at Longbourn. It belonged to Lady Catherine de Bourgh.

'I demand to see Miss Elizabeth Bennet!' shouted Lady Catherine as Lizzy ran from the house to greet her. 'Walk with me, young lady. I have much to say.'

Lizzy could not understand why the great Lady Catherine had

come to see her. Or why she looked so cross.

‘I have heard rumours that you are to marry to my nephew, Mr Darcy!’ she said. ‘Although I know this cannot be true.’

‘If you know it cannot be true, why have you come to see me?’ asked Lizzy. ‘It will make the rumours seem truer.’

Lady Catherine was not used to people talking to her so directly. ‘Do you care nothing for my nephew? Do you not understand how your family will drag his down by your connection?’

‘I am a gentleman’s daughter and he is a gentleman. So far we are equal,’ Lizzy replied.

‘But who are your relations? No one! If you marry, I will not see either of you again.’

‘That would be unlucky indeed,’ said Lizzy.

‘Tell me once and for all if you are engaged to Mr Darcy,’ demanded Lady Catherine.

Lizzy sighed. 'I am not.'

'And will you promise never to marry him?'

'I will not,' said Lizzy. 'Now I must ask you to leave.'

Lizzy's heart thudded in her chest as she walked away from Lady Catherine. Although any rumours that she was engaged to Mr Darcy were false, Lizzy now wished that they were true.

Chapter 15

As happy as Lizzy was for Jane, she could not shake off a feeling of sadness. Her sister was her best friend, and she could not bear to lose her.

Mr Bingley now visited often, and one day he came again with Mr Darcy. Elizabeth found herself joining the two gentlemen, as well as Jane and Kitty, on a walk. Finding herself side-by-side with Mr Darcy, Lizzy could not stay quiet.

'Mr Darcy,' she began. 'I must thank you on behalf of my family for

what you did for Lydia. They do not know it was you.'

'If you must thank me, let it be for yourself,' he replied. 'I did it for you. My feelings and wishes are unchanged. However one word from you will silence me forever.'

'Oh, *my* feelings are very much changed,' said Lizzy, laughing. 'I believe they are the exact opposite to what they were.'

The smile on Darcy's face at that moment would have shocked anyone who had ever thought him cold or proud.

Jane and Mr Bingley, and Lizzy and Mr Darcy were married. The Bingleys moved from Netherfield to be closer to the Darcys. They were the happiest of couples.

'I told you it would all work out,' said Mrs Bennet.

'Yes, my dear,' Mr Bennet replied. 'It seems you were right.'